THIS DREAM BELONGS TO

_ _ _ _ _ _ _

_ _ _ _ _ _

www.liberumdonum.com

The LIBERUM team dedicates this book to Juan Agustin, Isa, Gabi, Sofia, Valentina, and Samantha
- our new hero makers.
—J.C.

Dedicated with love to: Nola and Wren Dunton. May all your dreams be sweet.
—S.V.

Thanks to our KICKSTARTER backers, including:

Nastasha Baron	Maria Alcira Velez
Julio Alberto Calle	Maria Teresa Velez
Carmen Dapena	Erik Will
Mischa Dunton	

Immedium, Inc.
P.O. Box 31846
San Francisco, CA 94131
www.immedium.com

First hardcover edition published 2014.
Editor: Eric Searleman
Designer: Liberum Donum

Printed in Malaysia
10 9 8 7 6 5 4 3 2 1

Library of Congress Cataloging-in-Publication Data

Calle, Juan, 1977-
  Good dream, bad dream : the world's heroes save the night! / by Juan Calle and Serena
Valentino. -- First edition.
      pages cm
  Summary: "A father comforts his restive son by telling him that people all over the world
have imagined that heroes can help turn their bad dreams into good ones (with bilingual
Spanish translation)"-- Provided by publisher.
  ISBN 978-1-59702-103-6 (hardback) -- ISBN 1-59702-103-2 (hardcover)
  [1. Bedtime--Fiction. 2. Fear of the dark--Fiction. 3. Dreams--Fiction. 4. Heroes--Fiction. 5.
Hispanic Americans--Fiction. 6. Spanish language materials--Bilingual.] I. Valentino, Serena. II. Title.
  PZ73.C2883 2014
  [E]--dc23
                                    2014008732
ISBN: 978-1-59702-103-6

SUEÑO BUENO
GOOD DREAM,
BAD DREAM
SUEÑO MALO

The World's Heroes Save the Night!
¡los héroes del mundo salvan la noche!

BY
JUAN CALLE
&
SERENA VALENTINO

immedium
Immedium, Inc.
San Francisco, CA

"JULIO!" Papa called. "It's time for bed."

"I haven't finished searching for monsters!" cried Julio. He suspiciously glanced at his closet, positive that a creature lurked inside.

Papa chuckled, "You know there are no such things as monsters."

"¡JULIO! -dijo Papá- es hora de dormir."

"¡No he terminado de buscar monstruos!" contestó Julio. Sospechosamente observó el armario como si supiera que había una criatura en su interior.

Papá rió, "Sabes que no existen los monstruos."

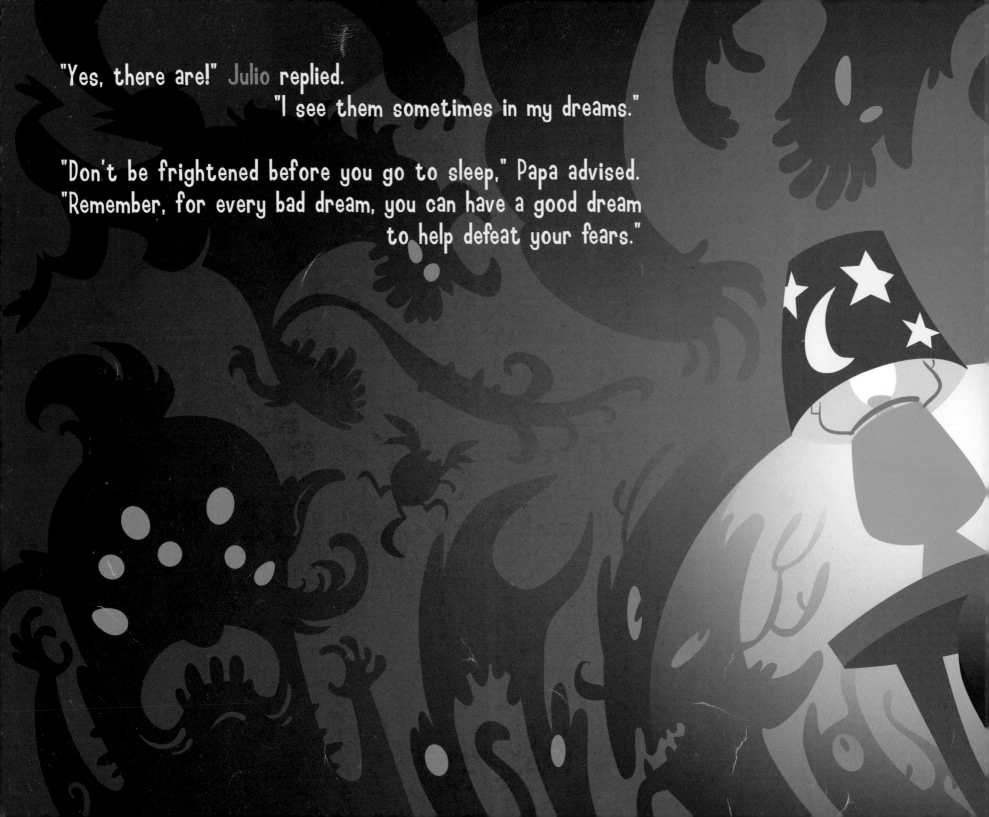

"Yes, there are!" Julio replied.
"I see them sometimes in my dreams."

"Don't be frightened before you go to sleep," Papa advised.
"Remember, for every bad dream, you can have a good dream
to help defeat your fears."

"¡Sí existen! -dijo Julio-
A veces aparecen en mis sueños."

"No te asustes antes de dormir -aconsejó Papá-
Recuerda, por cada sueño malo, hay un sueño bueno
que te ayudará a vencer tus miedos."

There will always be a mighty HUNTER
for every snarling MAMMOTH you may meet.

Siempre habrá un gran CAZADOR
por cada MAMUT enojado que encuentres.

And a crafty **FALCON**
for every scary **SCORPION!**

¡Y un artero **HALCÓN**
por cada temible **ESCORPIÓN!**

There is a strong **WRESTLER**
for each roaring **JAGUAR**.

AHUIZOTL

QUETZALCOATL

NAHUAL

Existe un fuerte **LUCHADOR**
por cada **JAGUAR** rugiente.

And there is a swift ARCHER
for every scowling CYCLOPS!

¡Y un raudo ARQUERO
por cada enojado CÍCLOPE!

A cunning **COMPANION**
for each devilish **SPIRIT.**

SUN WUKONG

ONI

Un astuto **COMPAÑERO**
por cada **ESPÍRITU** malicioso.

And a brave VIKING
for each angry TROLL.

Y un valiente VIKINGO
por cada iracundo TROLL.

There shall be an enchanting GODDESS
for every troublesome SNAKE.

Habrá una DIOSA cautivadora
por cada problemática SERPIENTE.

And a lionhearted WARRIOR
for each wild BEAST.

OBAYIFO

AMADLOZI

POPOBAWA

Y un arrojado GUERRERO
por cada BESTIA salvaje.

And a clever EXPLORER
for every creepy VAMPIRE.

VAN HELSING

MR. HYDE

Y un ingenioso EXPLORADOR
por cada repulsivo VAMPIRO.

There's a trusty ROBOT
for any invading ALIEN.

TITAN-O

ANAKIM

Existe un confiable ROBOT
por cada INVASOR espacial.

"Don't forget ME!" exclaimed Julio.

"Yes, indeed!" Papa laughed. "You are the mightiest hero of all!"

"¡No te olvides de MÍ!" exclamó Julio.

"¡Es cierto! -sonrió Papá- Tú eres el héroe más fuerte de todos!"

"Goodnight, my little dream warrior. Your imagination is powerful enough to conquer any nightmare. Sleep tight!"

"Buenas noches, mi pequeño guerrero de los sueños.
Tu imaginación puede vencer cualquier pesadilla. ¡Duerme tranquilo!"